STEEL GARDEN

poetry & stories

GiGi Huntley

Keychain Literary Press

CONTENTS

THE GIRL

Before
There was life
And it didn't seem fragile
You know?
I jumped and ran
And loved and thought I loved
And laughed and cried
And all the usual girl stuff.
Then
There wasn't.

When the waitress found The Girl, as everyone came to call her, it was just after the dinner rush had ended and the trash needed to be thrown out. She opened the gate to the dumpster and saw The Girl's shoe first. The shock made the woman unable to move for a few seconds and then she dropped the trash and ran back to the kitchen to grab the cook.

"Frank! Frank! There's a body out here!"

Frank was a large man, balding and grease-stained. In his forty-six years, the only dead body he'd seen was his aunt Patsy's, and that was at her viewing. He gently laid down the knife he had been using and followed the waitress.

He had a hard time sinking down to check The Girl's pulse, but he managed on his one good knee.

"She dead?" asked the waitress.

Frank nodded, still looking at The Girl. "Call the police, Tracy."

Tracy ran back to the diner, glad to be away from the body.

After the brief touch to her neck, Frank pulled away, but he couldn't help looking at The Girl. Her hair was the same mousy brown his ex-wife had always bleached-out and her open, staring eyes were a hazel-green, more green than brown. Her neck wore half of a 'best friends' necklace, purple finger marks and red scratches. The Girl's shirt was dirty, but there were blue-white patches that made Frank think somewhere there was a mom with a talent for laundry.

He felt like he had to stay with her, as if even her dead body needed protected. She was on her back, one arm outstretched to him. She had written her homework on her palm - "Read Ch12" - the letters were bubbly, happy, and Frank felt tears struggling to surface. He wiped them quickly away, forgetting the onions he'd been cutting would sting and redden worse than the tears. He winced at the pain, but he couldn't look away from The Girl. Her shorts were red and white, the kind kids wore for gym class. There was a number four on the right leg. He pictured her alive, playing volleyball, running. The shoes looked pretty expensive. Pale blue and white... The toes were scuffed, and he knew she had tried her best to get away.

Tears were stinging again, but Frank let them flow, sinking down against the dumpster gate, not caring about the bad knee.

The police were quick - the town only had two stoplights - and Frank tried to pull himself back together when he heard the siren. A quick prayer came to mind, surprising him. He used the chain-link gate to haul his heavy body off the ground and he gave The Girl one last sad glance before the cops were standing there, uncomfortable, not sure what to do first.

"Hey, Frank."

"Paul," Frank nodded back. They'd gone to high school and played football together thirty years prior, but this was the first time they'd done more than wave since. Paul always looked the other way when Frank drove home from the Stoplight Lounge after a few beers, and Frank always made sure cops got free coffee when he was on shift. Sometimes he'd even throw in free day-old pie.

"Um," Paul started as his partner pulled out a digital camera, "Tracy told dispatch you checked The Girl's pulse and she's definitely dead?"

Frank nodded again, although her open, staring eyes made that pretty obvious.

"Was her, um, skin hard?" Paul fidgeted. Usually, the sheriff handled this stuff. In the three years since he'd joined the force, he had never been this close to a dead human. He knew about rigor mortis, though, and that a dead deer hardened up too quick to let sit too long after a hunt.

"Gettin' there."

"Probably took her from somewhere a ways off and was heading up or down I-5 when he decided to dump her here."

Frank thought Paul was stating the obvious, considering the town was so small and neither of them recognized The Girl, but he muttered, "mm-hmm," in agreement.

A group was forming in the back lot, and Paul called in for backup to keep them away.

"Do we even have a coroner?" Frank asked, using his TV knowledge to have something to say.

Paul shook his head. "One's coming from Redding."

They both stared at Paul's partner, a young guy named Timmy or Tommy (Frank couldn't remember), as he took a lot of photos of the area and The Girl.

"She's really young, huh?" Timmy or Tommy looked up at the cook. Frank just sighed and nodded, wondering why they needed so many shots.

"How old do you think she is?" Timmy/Tommy asked, making his own odd version of small talk.

"Dunno," Frank muttered, looking after Paul, who had wandered over to the growing crowd. He was waving his arms, trying to contain them.

"She look familiar?"

"No," Frank was getting more and more pissed.

"Hmmm." The camera kept clicking.

"Do you need that many pictures?"

Timmy/Tommy looked up, surprised. He looked at the camera and back at Frank. "I guess not."

"Good. Can't we cover her? At least until the coroner gets here?"

"I don't think so... I think that might mess up the, um, crime scene or something."

Frank looked up at the cop again and realized he probably wasn't much older than The Girl and was looking younger by the minute. "Never mind then."

They stood there awkwardly, trying not to fidget. Another police car with its lights flashing showed up and parked between the people and the dumpster. Two more officers to wave their arms. Paul made his way back.

"Got the crowd somewhat controlled."

"Good, that's good," Timmy/Tommy said. Frank could only stare at a rock by Paul's shoe. The two cops continued to chat about trivial things. To Frank, it was like the static between radio stations. He found it hard to focus. He swayed a little, clutching at the chain-link.

"You okay, Frank?" Paul put a hand out and grabbed Frank's elbow. It was the first time they'd touched in three decades and neither was comfortable with it.

"I think I'm going to go clock out and head home. You know where to find me."

Every step away from The Girl was heavy with effort. Frank still felt a need to protect her. Instead, he forced himself through the gawking, questioning crowd and back into the restaurant. He saw the next shift's cook was already behind the order counter and he waved. When he entered the break room to clock out, the two waitresses that had just clocked-in were talking about The Girl.

"Hey, Frank. Tracy said you touched her. Was that weird?" Frank looked at the server's face and thought how much she looked like a small dog. Her cheeks were soft and stood out. Her nose poked up and flattened to her face. She wore her hair in two small pigtails at her neck. Funny, he'd once thought to ask her out and now he kept thinking about a Twilight Zone episode he'd seen as a kid, although it was blurry and he wasn't sure if it was something he'd made up or had actually seen. She smiled at him and he wanted badly to punch her or shove her aside, anything to make her dog-face quit smiling. Then he thought of the bruises on The Girl and hated himself. But the waitress's smile still pissed him off.

Frank tried to hide his irritation. "Why don't you two go to work, okay? There are a lot of people out there." He turned his back to them, rifled through the timecards, and clocked out without answering the question. He could feel their eyes boring a hole into his head, but didn't care. As he left, he didn't even glance their way.

He hurried to his car, thinking how nice it would be to get home and drink. A lot. Maybe drink so much he'd pass out and forget The Girl's eyes looking at him. A few miles down the road, he felt sick and pulled over just in time to throw up out the open window. He drove a little faster, anxious to pull into his dirt drive, wanting to lie down with the TV on too loud. His trailer loomed ahead. A single wide he'd bought after his ex had left. The property was his parents'—they lived half a mile away in the house he grew up in. Having no real lawn, Frank pulled up right in front of the trailer's door and yanked the handle so hard the coiled spring inside pinged off, never to be found again. He swore at the broken door, although he knew it was his own fault. Inside, he figured out a way to hold it just right so he could secure it. Normally, he wouldn't care about locking it, but the world felt less safe.

A beer. First a beer and then the TV. He swallowed half the can in the first pull and pushed the power button on the remote. Thankfully, he'd left it on ESPN. No chance of the news breaking in to talk about The Girl, although she was there in the room with him, anyway, her green-hazel eyes looking at him.

Another beer... No, something stronger. He checked the cupboard above the fridge. A half-empty bottle of Maker's Mark. That would work. He grabbed an old bar glass and poured out half of what remained of the bottle. He didn't even bother with a mixer. The first swallow burned, but it felt good. The second felt even better. He sat down and put his head back, staring at the ceiling.

The phone started ringing, and he ignored it. There was no way the coroner had made it in from Redding yet, and Frank knew Paul would make the drive out to get him. It wasn't a secret in town that Frank drank under stress and Paul wouldn't expect him to drive back into town. His first night after moving home, he'd gotten so belligerent he'd had to spend the night in jail. It was a surprise when it wasn't on the front page of the Siskiyou Daily News, the way everyone talked about it, pity heavy in their eyes and questions — "You gonna be okay, Frank?" "She was a piece of shit anyway, man, you're better than that and you know it, right?" "Just let me know when you're ready to date, okay?" Three years had passed, and he knew he should be over her leaving, but he wasn't. Now this.

He could have a kid about The Girl's age, if his ex hadn't had the miscarriage. They tried again and again to have a baby after that, but it never happened. Frank had thought it worked out for the best, with the divorce and all. He thought again of The Girl's mom, out there somewhere, praying her daughter was still alive. He took another desperate gulp of whiskey, trying to put the mom out of his mind, but she kept returning. In his imagination, she looked a lot like his ex-wife, maybe a little more classy, but blonde and pretty in an average kind of way. He saw the dad in his mind as a quiet pacing man.

He drank down the rest of the glass and grabbed another beer. The room was spinning, and he laid down on the sofa, watching SportsCenter and trying hard to concentrate on the words coming from the speakers' mouths. They laughed, but he didn't get the joke, and then everything got fuzzy and dark...

Someone was banging on the door. It made the trailer shake and Frank clutched at the sofa before realizing what was going on.

"Frank? You in there?" Paul called out.

"Yeah, hold on."

The bad knee ached and Frank had to half-roll off the sofa, something that almost made him sick. He shuffled to the door and was confused when it wouldn't open. Oh yeah, he thought, it's broken.

"Give me a sec, Paul." It took too long, but he managed.

"Hey, man, I hate to do this to you, but can I get you to sign some stuff? I brought it so you wouldn't have to come down to the station."

Frank motioned Paul in. He found a pen and his reading glasses and sat at the small table. Paul handed him a few sheets of paper and explained each one, and pointed at the highlighted areas to sign in. Frank had a flashback to when he and his ex bought their house. He shook it off and signed wherever Paul directed. The day was weird with memories.

"We're hoping fingerprints will i.d. her. There are quite a few missing girls along I-5 that fit her description, and we're not wanting all those parents coming in here getting their hopes up, you know?"

Frank did know, and he nodded without looking Paul in the face. They sat in silence for a bit, both staring at the fake wood grain marks on the cheap dining table. Paul spoke first.

"Makes me glad I had boys. Not that I don't worry about them getting into trouble, but I think it'd be worse having a girl."

"Yep."

"Worst part is, they'll probably never catch the bastard that did this to her. Might even be someone she knew." Paul stared at the beer bottles, not really seeing them. "When I finally decided to be a cop, my wife called it a midlife crisis. I told her nothing ever happens here aside from pulling drunks from the fair every August."

Frank just kept nodding along with the rhythm of Paul's voice.

"I'll keep you posted, okay, Frank?" Paul said as he stood to go. Frank was both afraid and glad that he was leaving. He didn't want to be alone with his own thoughts, but he didn't want to talk, either.

"Thanks, Paul."

He locked the door again, but wondered if he shouldn't just drive over to his folks' place and stay for a bit. His mom always loved him coming by for dinner and his dad was always happy for a game of Gin Rummy. He grabbed his keys and more of the beer and locked the door behind him. Minutes later, he rolled up to his childhood home.

He peeked in the window and waved to his mom, who was busy in the kitchen. She smiled and waved back, yelling, "Frankie's here, John!" He felt better already and was glad he had popped in.

Knowing what the answer was, he asked, "Got room for your only son at the dinner table?"

"Always!" His mom grabbed the beer and went to put it in the fridge.

His dad looked up from his chair, smiling, "Up for a card game, Frankie?"

"It's why I'm here, Dad." He pulled a deck from the desk under the front window and started dealing.

"Sad about that girl they found, huh, son?"

Frank felt his shoulders weaken as he fanned out his cards. "Yeah, Dad, it is."

Thankfully, that was the only time The Girl came up that night. He played three games of Gin Rummy and ate two slices of his mother's chocolate cake before drinking so many beers his parents insisted he stay the night in his old room. It was a sewing/guest room now, but it still felt comfortably familiar. Just what Frank needed. He slept a heavy dreamless sleep.

The next morning, he woke to his mom making sausage omelets and his dad shredding potatoes and cheese for hash browns. Frank offered to help, but his mom just told him, "This kitchen's crowded enough. You just sit down and read the paper. I'll get you some coffee."

The Daily News had a half-page picture of the fence around the dumpster with Paul pushing the crowd back with the headline: BODY FOUND! There weren't many other words, not that Frank looked for longer than a half-second. He flipped straight to the crossword, trying to make the morning normal again. "Hey, Mom, what's a six-letter word for 'without adornment'?"

"Simple?"

After breakfast, he played another game of Gin Rummy and ate one more slice of cake. He sat for a bit, watching some court television before saying goodbye. Like always, his mom kissed his cheek and hugged him. His dad told him to come back that night and they'd barbecue and Frank promised he would.

It was a short drive home. Frank sat in his truck, staring at the dust on his dashboard. His parents had always been so good to him. They had been proud of his C-average education, happy to cheer at every football game and help him with corsages and ties at prom. His mom cried at his wedding and at his divorce. His dad bought him a beer at his bachelor party and another when his ex left. He wondered briefly what their dreams for him had been when he was The Girl's age.

There were four missed calls and as many messages waiting for him inside the trailer.

"Hey, Frank, this is Polly Golden with the Siskiyou Daily News..." Frank deleted it.

"Hey, Frank, it's Polly again..." Another deleted.

"Frank? It's Tracy. Someone from the Daily News..."

"Hey, Mister, it's Lila. If you need the next couple of days off, just let me know." Lila owned the diner and had been a family friend for years. When he was a kid, she used to babysit him. After his divorce, when he'd lost his construction job in Medford, Lila told him if he was thinking of moving home, he might as well work for her. "I can never get anyone in here with a work ethic. Please, Frank?" He knew it was bullshit, but he appreciated her letting him keep his pride, and the last three years hadn't been too bad. She paid him okay and had offered to make him assistant manager. He was still thinking about that one.

He wondered what Lila had pictured him growing up to be back when she was babysitting. He shook off the question and called her back.

"Lila?"

"Frank! Hey, a bunch of news people from Medford and Redding camped out here and some reporter from the Daily News keeps coming around. I think it might be better if you take a couple days and let them lose interest. Tracy's lapping up the attention, but I know you don't really want that."

"Not really."

"So, I'll see you in a couple days?"

"That okay?"

"Don't worry 'bout us. You can make it up to me by taking the assistant job."

He managed a laugh. "Okay, okay."

"Good, it comes with a raise. See ya!" She hung up before he could protest.

The phone rang and he let the machine get it. "Frank, it's Paul..."

He grabbed the phone and interrupted, "Paul, hey."

"Hey, we gotta match on The Girl's prints. Her name's Mandy Green from some small town just past Grants Pass. Her mom's on her way to i.d. her."

Mandy. "Oh."

"She wanted to talk with you."

"What? Me? Why?"

"She wanted to talk to the person who found her..."

"But that was Tracy..."

"I know, but you stayed with her and I don't think Tracy'd do this woman much good."

"I don't know, Paul."

There was silence. Frank thought about The Girl—about Mandy—about her bubbly writing and scuffed-up shoes. He felt a pressure behind his eyes. Didn't her mom deserve someone better than him? But he was it and he couldn't let The Girl—Mandy—down.

"Okay. I'll do it."

"Thanks, Frank. Do you wanna meet her here or should I bring her by your place?"

Frank sighed. "Just bring her here. It'll be fine."

They said goodbye, and Frank stared at the phone as he hung up. The Girl's mom. What would he say? 'Sorry about your kid'? He sat on the sofa thinking about the pain his breakup had caused and how that was 1/100th of the pain this woman would be feeling. What about the dad? Where was he? Why wasn't he on his way with her? Even if they were divorced, he thought they should both be down here together. What kind of heartless bastard makes the mother of his dead kid come i.d. the body alone? He felt his blood pressure rise, so he flicked on ESPN.

After a while, he heard the crunch of gravel, but the car he saw out the window wasn't Paul's. An attractive woman in her thirties stepped out, and he opened the door, wondering how The Girl's mom had made the drive so quickly. Then he realized this woman seemed familiar.

"Are you Frank?"

"Yes."

"I'm Polly Golden, from the Siskiyou Daily News. I left a couple of messages."

"I got 'em."

She was smart enough to stay by her car. "Can I ask you a couple of questions?"

"There's nothing to say Mrs. Golden."

"Polly, please."

Frank shrugged.

She started again. "Maybe you could tell me how you felt when you realized The Girl was dead..."

"Well, how would you feel, Polly, if you found a dead girl thrown out like last night's trash?"

Polly looked shocked and then regained composure. "I guess I would feel sad..."

"Sad, pissed, wondering what kind of monster hurts a kid like that... Whaddya want me to say so you'll leave me alone?"

The woman stared at him. Not unkind, but not with pity, either. He couldn't make out the emotion on her face.

"I guess I'd be pissed, too. I'm sorry." She turned to get back into her car.

Frank softened. "You're just doing your job, I guess, right?"

She looked back at him. "Not really. I'm just the ad manager. The editor thought it would be better if a woman handled this story and all our reporters are men. He thought a woman would do a better job, get more of the story, but I feel like an ass, honestly." She half-smiled.

"I think I'd rather be ad manager."

"Trust me, begging people to place ads is much better than this."

"Yeah."

They looked at each other a second before she opened her door. "I'm sorry about this, Frank. I'll just tell the editor you refused to comment." She waved goodbye as she drove off in a dusty cloud, and he felt guilty that he enjoyed meeting her. He sat on the trailer steps a while, watching the dusty air clear, thinking about what a person should say to a woman who just had all hopes of her daughter being alive crushed.

The phone was ringing again. He couldn't believe it was already two o'clock. The day was moving so fast.

"Hello?" His hands were sweaty on the receiver.

"Frankie? It's Mom. Do you want steak or chicken for dinner? You're still coming for barbecue, right?"

"Yeah, Mom, I'll be there. Either's fine as long as you're making your sauce."

"Oh, it's already done."

He wondered. "Mom?"

"Yeah, Frankie?"

"The Girl from the dumpster..."

"Isn't it horrible?"

"Yeah... Well, I was there with her for a while until Paul got there and her mom's coming down to make sure it's her kid and..."

"Oh, the poor woman! I don't know what I would do if something ever happened to you. A mother should never outlive her kids!"

"Well, I might be a little late to dinner because she wants to talk with me... And, maybe if she's sad," he couldn't believe he'd said 'if,' "Could she get some dinner and stay in the spare room?" He worried he was asking too much, but there was no hesitation.

"Of course! I'll go put fresh sheets on the bed right now."

"Thanks, Mom."

"We'll see you tonight, then."

There was a slight pause and then Frank told his mother he loved her and could tell she might cry, so he hurriedly asked if there might be an extra toothbrush or if he should get one.

"We're going into town, Frankie. I'll pick one up for her. And flowers. She should have flowers..."

Frank felt better when he hung up, though he wasn't sure why. Probably The Girl's—Mandy's—mom would have someone with her and they would stay at the motel downtown or even drive back home tonight, but it felt right to feed her and offer her a bed to sleep in. It felt right that his mom should have the chance to comfort her. What didn't feel right was that there was a dead girl at the police station with eyes too stiff to close before her mother showed up.

The phone rang. His heart hurt. "Hello?"

"Frank? It's Timmy. Paul wanted me to call and let you know he's on the way with The Girl's mom." The young cop cleared his throat and swallowed. "It was pretty bad. She's all alone, too. We're gonna have to drive her home. She said her ex is on his honeymoon, and she couldn't get a hold of him when The Girl went missing. Shitty, huh?"

"Yeah."

"I can't believe no one else would come."

"Hey Timmy, I need to get cleaned up a bit. Thanks for calling and letting me know."

"Yeah, Frank, no problem."

Frank turned off the TV. There would be no last minute inspiration there. Any second now, the sound of tires on gravel would bring The Girl's mom to his door. What would he say? He sucked at this stuff. His ex had left him because he "couldn't communicate" and now he was supposed to sit alone with a grieving mother?

He wished he could grab one more beer, but he didn't want to be drinking when she showed up. He needed to be more in control. At the same time, he was glad for that case he knew was waiting in the vegetable drawer of the fridge. Just in case.

He thought about what people had said to him throughout the divorce, trying to help him feel better, and how he'd resented all of it. Lila had said the most with the smallest sentence: "I'm here." It had been a relief, and it was a relief now to know that he didn't have to say anything. This woman would not be comforted by any words, only by the golden potential of her dead daughter and what could have been. He realized it was a sick gift and that any parent would rather have their kid turn out to be a fat, divorced cook. He knew the only thing he could do for her was let her cry and nod and listen. He would offer her barbecue and a bed and his mother's arms full of whatever comfort they might bring.

He unlocked the broken door and waited. What else could he do?

And there it was, Paul's cruiser heading up his drive, the crunching of pea gravel harmonizing with the static in his brain that had returned. Frank thought he might die of a heart attack before the car stopped, but he didn't. His right foot was tingling, wanting to fall asleep. He shook it a bit and stood up, feeling heavier than he did when he had crawled out of bed that morning.

"Shit," he muttered to himself as he flung open the broken door. Paul got out of the car, gave him a grave, sad look, and walked over to the passenger door to let out Mandy's mom. Frank wasn't sure what he expected, but the dark-haired woman who exited wasn't it. His vision had been wrong. She wasn't blond at all. She was taller and curvier than The Girl, than Mandy. The eyes, though, those sad eyes that carried anger and sadness and confusion, they gave her away. Yes, this woman was definitely Mandy's mother.

Paul walked her up to Frank's trailer as Frank took a few steps to greet her.

"Frank, this is Sylvia Green. This is Frank McLaughlin."

Frank wasn't sure what to do. Sylvia stared at him with those full eyes. As if someone else took control, he took her in his arms, and she burst into tears. Paul looked at the ground, but his eyes were filling, too, and he cleared his throat twice.

"Why? Why did this happen?" she cried into his shoulder.

"I don't know," he said, that other shadow person still manipulating him, "We can't know."

He turned her around and moved her into his trailer. Paul didn't follow, and soon the sound of the car pulling away faded. Frank sat her down, grabbed a couple of glasses, poured what was left of the whiskey, added a bit of generic cola and some ice, and handed the glass to Sylvia. She didn't turn it away. She took a good swallow and quieted. Frank sat at his table, only feet away from her.

"She's a good girl. A good student... not the best, but more than average, you know? She was a track star. Colleges are looking at her... were looking at her," she gulped down more drink and looked again at Frank.

"I could tell that she had a mother who loved her," he said, feeling lame, "I mean, her clothes... were so white..."

His voice trailed off, but when he looked up at Sylvia, she said, "Thank you for noticing. Every time I was in a bad mood cleaning or doing laundry or whatever, I would remember that it was a way to show the world that Mandy was well-cared for, you know? Thank you so much for saying that."

She took a good long drink, draining her glass. Frank leaned back, opened the refrigerator, and grabbed a beer from the crisper. He popped it open and poured it into her glass.

"You're probably not really a drinker, but I am, and I'm sorry, but..."

She shook her head and sipped at the beer. "I only drink in restaurants, usually, but..." and she gulped down some more.

Frank couldn't help himself; he looked at this woman trying to gulp down cheap beer and smiled. Immediately, he felt ashamed, but she looked at him and once again shook her head before smiling too, an amazing grin that showed slightly crooked but very white teeth. She was beautiful.

"Please, I needed the smile. Mandy was such a happy girl. We laughed all the time. Maybe it's the alcohol, but I think she's here and willing us to smile. Is that dumb?"

"No. No, it isn't. It's the best thing I've heard today, actually."

Sylvia smiled again before tears started pouring down her face. She made a choking sound and then laid her head on the back of the sofa.

"I'm sorry," she said as she lifted her head, wiping tears with her palm. Her voice came out in a hoarse whisper, "She was my everything."

Frank sat at the table, feeling helpless as The Girl's mother shook with sobs.

He put down his beer can and stared at the table until Sylvia started hiccupping. Then he got up for a glass of water. As he handed it to her, he said, "I don't know what to do for you. Please tell me what I can do."

"You can be my friend."

He stood above her as she drank, and then took the glass, although she could have just as easily put it on the table. The trailer never felt smaller. He walked the couple of steps into the kitchenette, put the glass in the sink, looking out the window at the changing light.

"My parents live down the road and they have a spare room for you so you don't have to stay in a crummy motel. They'd like it a lot if we'd go over for dinner, but I understand if you're not hungry."

Sylvia was still, and he wasn't sure if she was thinking or about to pass out, but then she said, "Yes. I'd rather stay in a home than in a motel. Thank you. My car is at the sheriff's office. Can you take me there in the morning?"

"Yeah. I can. Of course I can."

She stood up. "Will you be staying there, too?"

Without hesitating, he said, "Yeah. I'll stay there, too."

She followed him out and watched him struggle with the broken door until he gave up, went into the trailer, grabbed a can of spaghetti sauce and used it to prop it shut.

"Luckily, there isn't anything out here anyone would want," he said. "My guns are at my parents' locked up." He didn't tell her it was because they were all worried he'd get drunk and shoot himself some night. She nodded. It seemed they were always nodding at each other. It was odd and agreeable at the same time.

He knew it was ridiculous to drive the half-mile, but his body couldn't handle the walk, so he said, "Do you mind if we drive? My knee..."

He opened the truck door for her—it felt strange after so much time had passed since he'd done it for his ex—and then got in himself. There was a lingering smell of the earlier vomit, and he wished he'd thought to open the windows earlier. He did it now.

It was only dusk, but the air was cooling and it was comfortable after such a long emotional day. They drove the few minutes in silence. It surprised Frank that it didn't feel awkward. In fact, he felt very real with her. As they pulled up to the house, she almost smiled again, making him assess it with fresh eyes. His mom had always believed in keeping a nice yard, so his dad worked hard even in his retirement to keep it spotless. The house was always painted before it needed it and every other week a window guy came out to shine up the outside. There were flowerpots on the porch stairs filled with bright red and orange mums to match the new fall season. It differed from the beat up trailer they let him dump on their property.

"You grew up here?"

"Yes, I did. It was a great childhood." He wasn't sure why he said it, but it was true. "I played football and my parents used to hang ribbons in those trees over there in my high school colors. They're great people. You'll love them."

He got out and noticed she waited for him to open her door. He didn't understand why, but he liked it and felt a little taller for it. They walked up the stone pathway side by side and he was glad. He felt like he needed to protect her, just like he had felt for Mandy earlier. A strange thought flashed through his head, "What if I had met them while Mandy was alive? Could I have kept her safe?" It was odd, and he shook it off. No sense in fantasizing about something impossible.

He opened the door, but his mom was already there. She had been crying and, being who she was, she took Sylvia into her arms and said, "I am so sorry, so, so, sorry." Sylvia cried on her shoulder, relieved to have this woman's comfort. When she pulled away, Frank pointed at his mom, "Mom, this is Sylvia; Sylvia, this is my mom, Anne."

"Thank you, Anne."

Frank's dad was standing at the corner of the foyer, waiting patiently. "This is my dad, John."

John handed her the flowers that Anne had picked out, "These are for you. Wish we were meeting under different circumstances." Frank almost felt relieved that his dad was uncomfortable. It seemed like someone needed to be at least a little. Despite that, though, Sylvia fit in. And why shouldn't she? The worst had happened. Everything else was minor.

Anne shuffled them to the living room, a warm, almost yellow room with comfortable but elegant furniture. Frank was glad that Sylvia could see he was from something better. He wanted her to feel as comfortable as she could.

"Do you have any clothes or anything?" his mother asked, and Sylvia looked embarrassed.

"I didn't think to grab anything. I just jumped into my car and drove here." She looked down at her hands. "I just remembered I forgot my purse at the sheriff's office..."

"Oh, John can give Paul a call and have that delivered," and before she finished the sentence, Frank's dad was heading to the kitchen line to get that set up. He was a man who liked to be necessary, and Frank realized watching him he was such a man, too. Being needed, being necessary was something he missed.

"Mom, want me to start the grill while Dad's calling Paul?"

"That would be great, Frank," she said, touching his arm before turning back to Sylvia. "Oh, why don't I show you the spare room? Do you want to rest before dinner? There's a small bathroom in there with a tiny shower stall, but there are clean towels and I think I have some clothes that might fit, if you'd like."

Frank watched as Anne directed a very thankful Sylvia and knew he was right to set this up. His mom was exactly what the shocked woman needed. When your brain shuts down and your heart is heavy, nobody could beat his mom at knowing how to comfort.

He wandered out back and started the grill. His dad joined him and put a hand on his shoulder, "Nothing could be worse, in my book. I remember when you got knocked-out during Pop Warner football when you were ten. I think my heart stopped until I saw you move again. It took all I had to get your mother to agree to let you keep playing."

"I forgot all about that."

"Yeah, luckily it was just a sore neck for a week or so, or your mom would have tied you to the shed or something."

They both chuckled, but Frank remembered a week spent in bed with his mom sneaking in when she thought he was sleeping to kiss his forehead and cry. He was even sorrier that he wasn't accomplishing more. He came from great people. Why wasn't he one?

"Here comes your mom," John said, giving her a sad smile as she walked over to them.

"Well, I convinced to her to take a warm shower and a short nap, but I'm telling you now that if she's sleeping when dinner's done, we are not waking her. That woman needs to sleep for days, if you ask me. Poor thing." Her husband reached out and held her with 50 years of love. Frank had to look away so they wouldn't see his tears. Today was the weepiest he'd been since infancy.

When he regained some composure while pretending to get the charcoal just right, he turned to them and said, "Thanks for letting her stay here. I just couldn't imagine her sitting in the dumpy Main St. Motel by herself, and there's no way she should be driving that many hours alone..."

His mom nodded. "About that, Frankie, I was thinking what if we gave you money for a bus ticket and you drove her back when she's ready? I don't think she needs that right now. I can't believe no one came with her today!" She wiped away a quick tear.

"Lila told me to take a few days right after I told her I'd take that assistant job she's been pushing on me, so I can do that," he said.

His dad put out his hand to shake, "Congratulations, Frankie! I always thought you'd be great running a business. You were always just quiet enough, you know, until you had to talk. I always told your mom that. When quiet men talk, everyone listens. I'm proud of you!"

And Frank knew he meant it.

His mom hugged him and said, "Well, that's exactly the news we needed today. A ray of sun through the clouds."

"You know you talk like a Norman Rockwell painting, right, Mom?" His dad laughed, and the sound filled a small hole in Frank's heart.

Sylvia was awake by dinner. Frank wondered if she'd slept at all. As his mom and dad readied the table, he asked Sylvia if she'd like to sit in the back for a minute. The sun was setting on this horrible day and, while he didn't say so, he thought maybe they should say goodbye to it.

Tomorrow wouldn't be much better, but at least today was done.

LAST DAY

Note to the reader:

While this story is about two people meeting and liking each other, it discusses depression and suicidal ideation. Neither are topics I take lightly, despite the lighthearted feel. If you or someone you know is having suicidal thoughts, you can call the U.S. National Suicide Prevention Lifeline at 988 any time day or night, or chat online at 988lifeline.org . Crisis Text Line also provides free, 24/7, confidential support via text message at 741741.

*****

Her last day at the office was unremarkable.

She sat at her desk, doing what she always did, thinking that something should set it apart from all the other days.

Nothing did.

At lunch, she changed it up and threw her apple and yogurt in the trash. She took the elevator five floors down and left the building, thinking of sushi.
*

The last day of his life was unremarkable.

He wasn't surprised, though. He woke up and started his farewell letter, thinking that something should set it apart from all the other days.

He paced. He cleaned. He packed. Why should he leave it for someone else? Then he imagined who would take on the responsibility. His mom? That thought made him pull magazines and journals from one box. He set them on fire in the fireplace he never used. The smoke filled the room, choking him. He ran for water, not realizing splashing the fine ashes would cause more smoke.

He had to leave. He took the elevator down ten floors and waved at the guard who sat at the desk.

He wandered around, unsure of how to spend his last day. Sushi sounded good. Might as well eat.

*

She only had one hour for her lunch. It made her laugh out loud - why care? Those people were "letting her go," "downsizing," "making drastic changes." She didn't need to go back. Ever. There were no photos on her desk, no postcards pinned to her cubicle. In five years, she'd never personalized her space, worried that any evidence of who she was outside of work would put her job in jeopardy.

She laughed again. The man walking behind her laughed with her, and she turned, fully expecting someone on his phone to glare at her.

"Sorry," he said. The man had been laughing with her. She smiled.

"It's okay. I'm sure it's hard not to laugh at someone laughing alone."

He shook his head. "Actually, I was laughing at a thought I had."

They laughed together and kept walking.

"I'm Daniel."

"Morgan."

She stopped at the sushi place.

"This is my stop. It was nice to meet you."

He laughed again. "This is my stop, too. Can I join you?"

As it left his lips, he wondered what compelled him to ask this sad-looking young woman to spend time with him. After all, he was planning on killing himself after dinner.

"Sure. Why not?"

Ordering was awkward.

"Spicy tuna, miso, and a Coke, please," he told the server.

"I'll have the same, thank you." She blushed.

That blush was intriguing to Daniel. He pondered it for so long that she blushed again and looked at her napkin.

"Sorry," he said. "I didn't mean to be rude by staring. I was kind of spacing out."

"No, it's..." She looked out the window.

"I was thinking about blushing and how I haven't seen someone do it in a while. Then I made it weird."

She stared at him, wondering about someone who could so easily explain his thoughts.

He continued. "Are you nervous now? Have I made you uncomfortable? It's just that I decided earlier this week to be more frank with people." He fidgeted and looked around the restaurant.

"No. I like it. It's surprising, though," she said.

The food came. Morgan hated to eat in front of others. Years of her mother's comments pounded in her brain like a migraine.

"What is it?" he asked.

Morgan sighed. "It's just that... I..."

"Just say it."

"Eating in front of people makes me anxious. I know; it's lame."

"Why do you feel like that?" he said.

She shrugged.

"Okay. What if I did this?" He picked up a small piece of ginger and stuck it to his chin.

She smiled. He liked it, so he did more. He spilled the dark brown soda on his crisp white French cuff. He rubbed seaweed into his teeth until it littered the spaces.

"Better?"

"Much." She reached over and wiped the ginger off his chin, before picking up her bowl of miso and slurping it loudly.

He applauded, forgetting his evening plans.

Years later, he would tell her she saved his life by slurping soup with him.

MY VALUE

"I want what I want!" The girl sat in my chair, yelling at her mom, demanding that I now straighten the hair I had just spent over an hour curling per her original idea. It was homecoming.

"Okay, okay!" Her mom, a woman in her mid-40s with unfashionable jeans and a short blonde bob, was literally ringing her hands. I thought that only happened in Victorian novels.

"I'll need a minute to contact the client I have scheduled at 3:30..." I was trying to broadly hint to this woman that her daughter was being a bit of a brat and that she needed to take control of the situation. It wasn't working.

"Okay, that works."

"And I'll need my hair washed again," the brat whined, "because there's so much hairspray in it."

I wanted to tell these people to go screw themselves, instead I texted my next TWO clients to push them out another 90 minutes. I offered them each a discount, too, quietly cursing my luck. Why did I take a new client today?

"Okay, let's get it washed."

"Maybe use a toning shampoo to brighten it a bit? Elise was just saying her hair seemed brassy." I just gave her a thin smile and motioned for the teen to head to the sink. I quickly washed and conditioned her hair (with non-toning product).

"I'm going to use the hood dryer to give her a head start, since her hair is so thick and long." The girl was too busy on her phone to even care.

"That's fine. I'm going to run and get her a latte."

It ended up taking longer. When I finished, my next client had been waiting for ten minutes. She was giving me the OMG eyebrows, too, watching the brat whine to her mom that she should have kept it curly.

Her mom pulled out her card. "So it's $50, right?"

And something in me snapped, and I said, "It's $50 an hour for specialty hair, so it's $125."

"Oh, okay." She reached back into her wallet and pulled out a different card. I ran it and turned the tablet to her for her signature. She left me a $5 tip, of course. As they were leaving, I heard her mom say, "Next time, you're doing your own hair."

The other stylist, Cindy, had been sitting at her station, waiting to see how it played out. She turned to me and said, "$50 an hour, huh?"

"Yep, I'm updating my website and social media right now," I was typing it in while my client, a good friend, roared with laughter.

PUBLIC OPINION

She shifted in her seat, her right hip starting to ache, but she was still listening. His heavy words made the air as dense as fog.

It was done.

They'd tried grieving the loss of their child—just another casualty in just another shooting—together (and with millions of onlookers hitting send after announcing their opinions on why. As if why could heal them.).

He finally finished, and she realized she'd been nodding along to the rhythm of his voice. Her head still softly bouncing, she stood and looked away, not sure who should leave their house.

On the wall, a family portrait. They should have got their child a dog. A golden retriever to round out the family of three in that picture would have been nice. But, no, that dog would wonder what happened, just as she did.

He followed her eyes to the wall and looked away.

He would do the leaving. The house was cluttered with constant reminders he didn't want. A do-over. He needed a do-over.

She sat back down.

Her hip moved from an ache to a stab, but she didn't move. Letting the pain go was unimaginable.

TAROT CARDS

"I've been messaging the guy I dated in high school."

I'd just started painting bleach onto the first foil, so we had plenty of time to work through this.

"I'm guessing that your husband loves that."

"It's terrible, but you know how things have been between us."

"You were going to bring up counseling..."

"I did, and he said, 'I don't need therapy, but feel free to fix your issues.' Nice, huh?"

"Ugh. That's bad."

"Yeah..." Linda was quiet, and I let her be while folding more foil into rectangles around her face. "His name is Brett. The high school boyfriend. He's still in California."

"Did he get married and have kids, too?"

"Married, yes; kids, no. He wants some, though. She doesn't."

"Sounds like there are some feelings there. What are you going to do?"

"I don't know. The twins are thirteen now. They could handle it if Steve and I break up."

"Is that what you want? What would be your best-case scenario?"

"I mean, the best case would be Steve showing me some fucking affection, you know? Best case would be a conversation. Honestly, he checked out a long time ago, not that it's a good excuse for me and Brett checking in all day like we do."

I was glad it was one of those nights where the other three stylists were gone already.

"We need wine for this talk. Are you up for a glass? I already locked the door, so no one will bother us." I was already headed to the refrigerator in the backroom. "Also, I need more foil. I always forget how much hair you have."

"Wine sounds excellent," she got up to follow me. "I have to make some kind of change, Rebecca. I can't live like this. It's been years. I mean, the girls barely need me. They're in high school."

"Red or white? Or whiskey?"

"White." I poured us each a large glass.

"Okay." I started ripping foils. "Say you leave Steve. Would it be to head to California? Do you and Brett have a future there? Do your parents still live in your hometown? Will the girls go with you? If they do, won't they be angry with you about leaving their friends? Or do you leave, because you deserve better, and you make a life here for you and the girls? Don't tell me you haven't thought through the different scenarios."

I pointed toward my station, and we wandered back, drinking as we walked.

"I have. I won't lie. I'd stay here for the girls. And, if Brett decides to leave his wife, we can decide later what to do about geography."

I started going through her hair again. "That makes sense. I just wouldn't want you to leave Steve *for* Brett. You've been unhappy for a long time, but let's not tie our happiness to another person so quickly."

"I know. It's just fun to feel wanted again."

"I get it. Who doesn't want that?"

"Did you like your divorce attorney?"

"I did. I'll text his info to you. I especially liked that he was a really tall man with wide shoulders, so my ex had to look up at him when they met." We both laughed, but there was a serious note to the evening.

"Do you think Steve has someone?" I asked.

"Like, is he cheating?"

"Yeah. Or could he be depressed or something?"

"He's mean, actually. The girls and I are the depressed ones in the house. Maybe he does have someone. It might explain why nothing we do is right lately. Maybe he's mad that he's there when he could be somewhere else. Mallory asked me the other day if he was tired of us. Isn't that sad?"

"It is. I'm sorry for all of you right now. The girls are old enough to feel when things are weird at home."

"Should I just ask him?"

"Yeah, but not right after I do your hair! He'll think I put thoughts in your head!"

"Did he say anything to you when he came in a few weeks ago?"

Uh oh.

"Um... We don't talk about you or the girls, to be honest, and this makes me a little uncomfortable. I'm the neutral third party, remember?"

"Ugh! Do you go home at night and laugh at what you know about people in town?"

"Not really. Not usually, anyway. But sometimes I cry driving home."

She turned and looked at me, making me have to redo a foil. "Really? We're that bad?"

"No. I'm kidding. I mean, I've had clients die, so, yeah, I've cried about clients, but I learned twenty years ago how to ground myself and not take all of your stuff home with me. It took me a while."

"How did you do it?"

"You really want to know?" She nodded slightly as I finished the left side of her head. "I worked with a psychic."

"Really??"

"Yeah. It wasn't planned. I worked with this woman who ran her phone bill up to almost $2,000 by calling the Psychic Friends Network back when everyone had landlines..."

"We're the same age, Beck. I remember the Psychic Friends Network." She rolled her eyes and took a big sip of wine. I paused and grabbed my glass.

"Yeah, yeah, anyway, I was her secret Santa and thought it would be fun to get her a reading with a real psychic, so I looked in the back of the Weekly and found one - Phoenix Sinclaire."

"Sounds made up."

"Duh." I downed the rest of my wine and went back to foiling the right side. "While we talked on the phone, I pictured her looking a certain way - black curly hair, short, a white turtleneck under a denim jumper - you know how you can 'see' the people you talk to at a call center? I could 'see' her. Anyway, I told her about my co-worker, how she ran up this bill, how she was religious, so I wanted to make sure that this would be a good fit, before I gave her the gift certificate. So Phoenix said, 'Why don't you come over?' I said, 'Right now?' And so I drove to the East End and rang her doorbell - she worked out of her condo - and when she opened the door, she looked exactly like I imagined her."

"Weird!"

"It was! So I'm staring at her for a half-second, and she says, 'Oh, you're one of us! Come in!'"

"Oh, wow, Beck!!"

"Yeah! So I walk into this very nice, but normal, apartment and we sit and have tea together, before I say I'd like to get the gift certificate. She says, 'Why don't I do a reading for you? A free one, so you can tell her about the experience?'"

"Fun!"

"So she pulls out her tarot cards from a box on the table. They were wrapped in soft purple velvet. To be honest, I tried not to smile, because my mind wandered to the Crown Royal bags, which is probably why I can remember the purple bag at all. So, anyway, she has me hold the cards to my heart with both hands. 'Close your eyes and focus on what you want to know - the answer to any question or whether you'll get your heart's desire.' So I do exactly that. Then she has me shuffle them. As I'm shuffling them, she tells me to hand her any cards that call to me, so I handed her ten separate cards. She laid them out on the table and started staring at them with a serious face."

"What did she say?"

"That I was in transition, that my old self had died and I was reborn, that I would have great love and make money."

"And it's coming true! I wish someone would read my cards."

"I just have a few more foils, and then I will."

"Really??"

I smiled and quickly finished up the section I was on.

"More wine? And I'll get the cards."

She jumped up and clapped her hands like a kid. "Yes! Yay!"

We refilled the glasses, and I grabbed my cards from my bag.

"You keep them in your purse?"

"Sure. Why not?"

She looked surprised, and I laughed. "No, I'm kidding. I put them in there, because another client asked if I knew anyone who read cards, so here they are."

"I'll pay extra! Just tell me what you charge," she told me as we sat across from each other at the reception desk.

"You can tip me extravagantly." I pulled them out of the box and shuffled them before handing them over. "Okay, hold them in both hands toward your heart and think about what you need to know. When you feel ready, shuffle them however you like and hand me three. We'll do a simple spread. If you have questions, we can always draw more cards."

She pulled the cards, soft with age, to her chest.

"Close your eyes. Now, try not to point to what you think you need. Just hold your question and focus on it. Allow the cards to find the truth without your help."

She opened her eyes and started moving the cards around on the table. They were big, so she shuffled them by moving them into circles and folding them together. She paused three times to pull cards.

"These stood out to me."

"Okay, let's see what we have." I put the cards down facing her. "Some readers do reversed readings, but Phoenix told me that I could choose not to and the cards would read as they should, so I've never done it. I don't like to bring the negative into the moment. Your first card represents your past or the foundation of your question. You gave me the goddess Isis who stands for Magic. This card represents you at the beginning, a woman who is creative and strong, who knows she is powerful. This is a good foundation."

She stared at the card. I handed it to her. "Get your phone and take a picture. You need a reminder of who you were and still are. Make it your home screen." She quickly did exactly that.

"This is giving me goosebumps, Beck."

"It should! You should see the truth of yourself. These cards are just a tool - you're the one creating the reading." I pointed at the second card. "See this? The Six of Staves? It represents where you are right now. What do you see when you look at this card?"

She shifted uncomfortably, afraid to get it wrong. I handed her the card.

"Um, she looks happy...?" I nodded. "She's got this crown on her head and she's riding this fancy horse... She looks like royalty or something." She looked back at me, needing some feedback.

"You're right! She's the winner and gets to ride through a parade that was created for her."

"But I don't feel like a winner right now."

"Don't you?"

She looked at me, a foil halo surrounding her face.

"No. I mean..."

"You have two men in your life, your daughters are happy and healthy, you have the money to get these highlights, you drove here in a new Audi, your flower shop is on the front page of a local magazine... Do I need to go on?"

She sat back, staring at the card.

"My life is pretty great, huh?"

"I know that your husband is going through something. It might mean that he won't always be in your life, but YOUR life is on track, my friend," I smiled. She looked relieved.

"Okay, what does the next card say?"

"If you don't change anything, if you continue on as you are, you're going to get some exciting news. See how these are being delivered like arrows? They're moving quickly. You're going to get a phone call or message that could change your life..."

Just then, her phone rang. We both jumped. She laughed, but her eyes were wide.

"Hello?" Her face went white almost immediately. "Oh my God, okay, I'm at the salon. Let me get this out of my hair, and I'll be right there." She started talking faster than I'd ever heard her. "That was Rory. She said Steve passed out while they were at his mom's house for dinner. She called 911. They think it's a heart attack. I need to get to the hospital!"

I pointed to the sink. "We need to get the color out of your hair." I started pulling foils and shampooing.

"The cards were right! I got... Oh my God, Rebecca, I can't imagine my life without him." She was sobbing while I rinsed the lather from her hair. It was golder than I wanted, something my brain couldn't help but think after years of assessing color, so I ran some toner through it.

"Sit there with that on your head. I'm going to get your stuff together." She sat there with her hair in my sink, crying so hard. I put everything together, including my own things. "Okay. I'm going to rinse this, towel dry it, and then I'm driving you."

"No, you don't need to do that!" I was already drying her with a towel. "I need to pay you..."

"Stop it! It'll be impossible to find parking in that stupidly small lot, so let me take you to the ER door. You can pay me when we fix this." She nodded as I quickly braided her hair. I shoved her out the door, locking it behind us.

TRAILER TRASH

Outside, the rain beat pockmarks into the asphalt, and inside it beat identical holes into my brain. Living in a trailer when a storm hit was like living in a kettle drum.

It was better than the few weeks I stayed in a tent, though, and I was dry at least. I had a house once. Nothing exceptional, but it was mine, and it had a permanent address nailed to the front porch. Now my address contained the words "lot #26" - the number painted in fading golden yellow on the blacktop my travel trailer was parked on.

I sat at my dining table/sofa/bed and tried to read, but the hammering was too much of a distraction. I leaned over to the small fridge and grabbed a soda - it was too early for beer - and leftover pizza. Without getting up, I popped the pizza into the microwave, wondering if I'd be able to hear the ding over the rain. It didn't really matter, I watched it for the full fifteen seconds, anyway.

As I chewed and drank, I thought about everything that led me here, to the Sunshine Corral Trailer Park. There was the collapsing economy (duh), but my luck had turned far before anyone else's, so I didn't want to jump on that bandwagon. No, I think it was a bunch of stuff. The breakup and having to pay my ex-boyfriend off to keep the house was a biggie. Then the roof literally fell in, and I drained all credit cards to repair it, my insurance not being as "full-coverage" as I had thought. Then the new boyfriend, the one with no job, who stuck around until I lost mine...

Fuck it. I reached for the beer. This probably wasn't the best thing, wallowing. What would it change? I decided to put the table up and pull out the bed. Might as well go all the way and climb back under the covers. Would the rain ever stop? Seriously.

WHAT IF

She noticed a pattern of red and orange.

Pillows on a brownish-red sofa - all different shades of red and orange. The woodwork - a golden brown, almost rusty. Area rug - yellows fading into mustard, browns burnished garnet.

Even the people talking seemed to have a sunset glow about them. She decided it had to be the lighting.

She sipped her coffee and watched everyone in the shop.

There was a couple breaking up in the corner. She could tell by the way the man's eyes looked everywhere but at the woman across from him, and how the woman could only look at him, eyes glazed over, mouth slightly open, shoulders slumped in defeat as she listened to him rambling. She willed the woman to get up, throw her drink on the man and leave, but the woman had turned to stone.

There was a business woman taking up a large table with her papers and laptop. Probably used to a big desk. She watched the woman in her grey suit juggle the p.c., coffee, and cell phone, but that got boring after a while. She found herself staring at the vein on the woman's forehead more than anything else, so she looked away.

There was a young family dressed in REI's best. Even the jog-stroller looked casually expensive. She imagined the conversation:

Dad: *I thought we decided to get the sustainable disposable diapers?*

Mom: *I told you, the cloth ones are better, less waste.*

Dad: *Look, we talked about this already, at least the disposables break down, the cloth diapers use too much water to clean...*

Mom: *You're right, you're right... but I already bought the cloth ones!*

She smiled and took another sip. Then she saw him. She wasn't the only people-watcher in the shop. He smiled and raised his paper cup at her. She had to laugh. He nodded his head to the business woman and rolled his eyes. She laughed again and looked at the young family. He nodded, smiling. The breaking-up couple awkwardly got up to leave. She and her co-conspirator watched them shuffle out. She glanced back at him, suddenly sad.

Then she put on her jacket, gave him a small smile, and left.

ABSENT

silence can never be misquoted
but it can mean very different things

i have nothing to say
i have nothing to say to you
i have nothing to say that matters to you
i don't care

ACCIDENT

when the paint dries
she traces the texture
with her fingers
not just one
but all of them
she remembers each trench
like the curve of a riverbed
she's followed

which stroke was planned
which one an accident

did it matter

ACHY

it was the longing
the ache
that made her realize she was alive at all
without it she was a mechanical machine
turned on
turned off

the pain reminded her
she was a woman
soft
hard
hot
cold
wanting
longing
it threatened her life
threatened to derail her
to hurl her over a cliff of safety
into darkness and rushing water
sweet
exciting
fresh
a current she didn't know how to navigate
pushing her to an unknown sea
and she longed to jump

to disrupt her cautionary tale
her sample-sized life
her snippet
to discover that she was
technicolor
a symphony
something one cannot escape
someone not to be forgotten
the longing
the pain
the want
deserved to be shared
unleashed
it was cramped up inside her
feeding off her imagination
bloated from her fantasy
wishing to corrupt her by caressing her skin
instead of languishing in the dark parts of her soul

ALIVE

the idea
that there were people
who didn't know
she was dead
made him happy
she was alive
to someone out there
he liked that

ALONE

solitude means alone
there is no solitude
with a smartphone in your hand
the echo chamber is not your own voice
your own ideas
sometimes you have to seek answers without cell service
without likes
or hearts
or smile emojis
let the battery die the answer is not there
if you must write
pencil and paper and a park bench
a picnic table of scratched-in graffiti
is all the input you need this time

AVERTED

if you didn't know their politics
you'd pull over and fix their flat
but that bumper sticker told you
all you need to know

AVOIDING

how long is this going to take

always impatient or maybe needing to steel yourself

as long as it needs to i guess
or we can skip it altogether
we gave it a try right
i'd hoped to be important
to impart something
to be one of the voices in your head
but i'm not
so let's not bother i guess

BLANK

a box of
empty notebooks
made him laugh

it was so like her
to
collect blank pages

wasn't that why
she chose him

BLARING

the quiet
made it
difficult
to sleep

especially
with the
noise inside her head
at full volume

BOMBARDED

what a shame
that letting our minds
wander
isn't like a beautiful
meander
through flowers and shrubs
so often we have to
bat away thoughts
like mosquitoes

BOUND

close the door
turn on the light
time for conversation
not the speech that you prepared

this isn't just happening to you

CLUTCHING

like gatsby
she fell for a facade
a glorious dream life
and like him
she did everything she could
to get it

the difference

once it was hers
she didn't want to
share it so shallowly
she wanted to keep it

all to herself

CRANKY

when her back hurt
she tried
to think positively
like

at least i'm alive
to feel this pain

but her back didn't like it
so she stopped

curious

she knows herself well
and still has to push aside
the morbid curiosity
about how others view her
which shouldn't matter

they couldn't know
how she worries
or the freckles on her
finger and toe
and that she cries
about the world
and her own body

how could they

CUTTING

the truth
is like a diamond
multifaceted
with the appearance of transparency
angles can be shaped
but the edges
are sharp enough to cut
whoever dares
to handle it carelessly

DECISIVE

she held the two shirts up
and
looked in the mirror
tipping her head
to fit above the collar

the blue? or the red?

he barely glanced up
um, i guess the red

she decided on
the blue

DELICATE

her delicate unease
manipulates her
pushing her down
her face in water
drowning
can't escape
heart hurts
breath caught
not easy
sorry

mentally liquidating to minimize distraction
her brain dumped out on someone else's table
her heart thrown in the corner to gather dust and
to house insects who harbor no bad feelings

DIFFERENT

climbing trees
as a child
fearless
as you go
higher
and higher
to where the view
is your town
but different somehow
a glimpse of
adulthood
seeing the same thing
and having it changed

DISTRACTED

the words did distract
she made them real
important

she was careless
with her body
with her heart
she let them lead her
down a seductive path
she tripped
and fell
the bruises would heal
the scars would remain

DOUBTFUL

she and the cat
stared out the window
there was a bird
that looked like a robin
but she was doubting herself
it looked rounder
its orange chest more copper
her cat kept chirping like
it was speaking the bird's language
the bird tipped its head
bobbing to look for worms
not knowing the drama
behind the glass

DOUBTLESS

as she watched him sleep
she realized that she missed him
she missed herself a little too
she missed the version of herself
that made people look a little longer
than a glance
she missed him
standing closer when he saw
someone talking a little too long
and she missed him kissing
her much sharper shoulders
she didn't miss the wondering though
she knew now with no doubt
that he loved her

DRAMATIC

reacting to drama
is not creating drama
human emotions
just are
let it out
or
like a cancer
it festers
crying is good
anger is normal
sadness is inevitable
release
unleash
be human
let it all go

DROWNING

after he rearranged
the deck chairs
he went downstairs
and made a tea
out of lemon rinds
and honey
sipping the hot water
he watched
the cold
as it covered his shoes

DULL

once she painted her face
red lips
black eyes
but no longer

once she didn't walk
she danced
and people noticed

her smile seems unreal in pictures

now she's taken to
barely turning up the edges
when once her teeth blinded

EARTHY

the smell reminded her of something
some other time
it was gum
she suddenly remembered how that first boy
chewed cinnamon gum
all the time
he also smelled of the woods
around his house
pine and sap
some kind of earthiness
that layered over the scent of the gum
and the detergent his parents kept
in boxes that piled up in the laundry room
as if they were worried the world would run out

EASY

words were easy
they came to her
unbidden

it was meaning
that sometimes
skirted around a
corner
laughing
knowing that
without it
the words were
nothing

EMPTY

the sidewalk was hot
and she walked with a hop
wishing she'd
slipped on some shoes
before running to the mailbox

her buzz was gone

and the box was empty

fuck

she wanted to stand
and wait for the mailman
but she didn't want blisters

EXPERIENCED

it was amazing how many people
told her she was wrong
about her own identity
it was getting tiring
no
it was past tiring
and bordering on insane
her decades of experience
just existing
put down by someone else
who couldn't know
that her nationality
was not something
for them to decide
she knew who she was

FIERY

when the panic comes
it wakes you
consumes you
fills your chest with
burning
and your mouth with
acid
your breathing becomes
a chore
and your mind becomes
the enemy

FILLING

the paint hit the wet paper and bled out
almost a circle
she watched the deep tone glide to the edge
leaving an icy pastel behind
like a ghost
like an imprint
like the past
the past
there were moments she wished didn't stay
but they existed in pale
those shadows
following her to the edge
filling up her center
like anxiety filling an ulcer

FINE

she suddenly believed
everything
would be okay
for one moment
the anxiety
vanished
replaced with
complete faith

the future
would sort itself out
today was fine

FIVE

she liked to keep
her regrets
to a minimum

maybe five

she knew
if she thought
too hard
more would appear

so
yeah
five

FRAUD

to pretend
you pulled yourself up
by your own bootstraps
is laughable but yes
continue the narrative
the truth is still the truth
regardless of your fiction
to pretend
you champion survivors
when you turned your back
is laughable but yes
profit off your story and tears
the truth is still the truth
regardless of your fiction

FRUSTRATED

it feels like
everyone else
succeeds
and i stay the same
no forward progress
even the bad people
people who hurt others
and lie and
fake like they care
i watch the initials
added to their names grow
and wonder why
bad people
always win

FUNNY

she wondered if she was a secondary character
she didn't feel like the protagonist
wouldn't she be sexier
or
at least
more interesting
she felt like she was there to prop others up
the lead would be more dynamic than that
her wardrobe would be different
better
she'd use more hand lotion
and special eye cream

she hoped she was the funny side kick at least
someone the audience looked forward to seeing

GIFTED

she collected boxes of matches
not from bars
or anything like that
she hunted gift shops for them
any fancy store
full of candles
had stacks of them
for sale
she would slide the prettiest one
into
her
purse
then she would buy the most expensive
candle in the place
and have it gift wrapped

GRACEFUL

he jumped a fence
with such grace
as to make her heart pause

it was like he floated over
slowly
the strength in one hand
enough to hold himself
with ease

could he
do the same
with her

GREY

all my rock heroes
are grandparents

i see
their grey hair
and am
oddly calmed

we all soften
we all age

if we're lucky

HARD

the crunch of gravel
under tires
always meant home
to him
for her
it was a reminder
that she deserved
more
someday
he would search
she would search
different roads
for different people

HELPFUL

she dared him to be happy
she pushed him to it
screaming hysterically
she wouldn't allow him not to be
oh
how he pushed back
he would allow the black clouds
to gather
the lightning
to strike
he would roar back at the thunder
and then she would hand him a towel
a tumbler of whiskey
and get the fire started

HOPE

never mind she thought
we are not the ones
who push beyond
every day your life is plotted
like a field of landmines
we carefully maneuver around
losing
dignity here
happiness there
like limbs detached
you would have been another loss
she thought
she wondered
what if
for a moment that never was

ITCHY

how can i show you
they don't matter
their poisonous words
merely mosquito bites
itchy but not permanent
that false friends
will be replaced
by love so big
nothing can contain it
and this sadness they've thrown at you
will be tomorrow's story you tell
laughing
that you gave small people power
over someone as magnificent
as you

JEALOUS

the hard part is what happens in her own head

the endless chatter
the judgment

she almost envies
the people who never
dissect
their actions
who never
review
what they've done
or said

it must be nice

KNOWING

it was that moment
fingers close to touching
for the first time
when she felt time slow
colors were bolder
around her
the wind was soft
she memorized all of it
each half-second recorded
it was the start of their story
together

LESS

oh comparison
you stab me
jab me
and make me
feel
less than

LIAR

the restaurant smelled
like 1993
winston lights
with tequila
and cheap domestic beer

she hated it

and he loved it

so she smiled
and said
she did too

LONELY

she heard the man
weaving
tall tales
revising history
to make the stories
better
and suddenly realized
he was lonely
so she leaned in
and
listened
more intently

MADDENING

asking more questions
than can ever be answered
and
resisting being conformed
into perfection
sounds like the work
of a genius
and artist

and it is

an intelligent madman
and a starving artist

seldom does it bring comfort and wealth

MESSY

perfect
was never the goal
she liked messy

storms with clouds so quick
they outpaced the crows

and sweaters with holes
in the elbow
worn by too many people to count

a crooked smile
and a hint of rascal

MINGLING

he crushed out the cigarette
wishing it would be his last
knowing it wouldn't
the plane was
smoky enough
without him lighting another
so he waited
feeling sorry for the row
in front of him
the non-smoking section
he wondered how they could stand flying
with the cloud of
others' stress
hovering

MISSED

yesterday
there was still hope
he was still here
and everyone could imagine
he would be for a while

today
there is an empty chair
that was his
and she didn't know
that a body could make so many tears

MURDEROUS

the monster
was feeding
poking
and
laughing
until she pushed it
out the window
and
shut the blinds

OLD

she looked at old pictures to remind herself
that she was beautiful once

she'd never relied on her looks
but she knew at one time
that she could smile
and get a door held open
or a drink delivered in a bar

who knew that she could miss something
she'd never considered at all

PAINED

no cap to grief
take your time
i don't know your story
you don't know mine
your heart hurts
okay
i know you'll be there
when it's mine someday
time doesn't heal emotional wounds
your soul isn't like skin and bones
so cry and rage
lightning and thunder
i'll be here to pull you out from under
your pain

PAINTED

every night she paints
what looks like blobs to others
for her
though
a whole world comes alive

colors and textures
could be flowers or trees

or nothing that exists
in real life

and that was the point

PATIENT

the airport chairs
were hard
but he attempted
comfort
as he waited

he stood
pacing
in between
sitting with head in hands

he was tired
but he would wait

PICKY

the smell bothered her
it was bacon
and cigarettes
a hint of cat pee

the property manager handed her
an application

it's a fifty dollar fee to check your credit
we take venmo and paypal
no personal checks

hmmm

she stood in the sad small kitchen
the burners were tilted
not one parallel to the range's surface

the deposit is $1350

will it be cleaned

the property manager looked around
um
sure

she peeked into the bathroom
the toilet was brown at the water line
and the grout on the floor
crumbled at its base
she was afraid to look in the shower stall

she handed the paper back

that's okay
i'd rather sleep in my car

PROMISING

a million years ago
i owned a house

when i lost the house
and moved
they dug up my garden
the place my baby laughed
but it was better than
throwing grass on it like a grave

they took the porch
where she used to play
and put down concrete steps
no more swing tied to the tree branch

alcoholism was the mistress in the closet

i left that husband
but the mistress got my house

i drive by
no garden
no porch
no swing

the people there don't know
that i talked to the walls
promising the house
things i couldn't deliver

i hope it understands
that i tried

PUNCHY

it's not hard to make someone hate you
a flag in front of your house
letters on a hat
a bumper sticker
a 24/7 news cycle and a video recorder in every pocket
pick your angle
echo
safety security
you're living in fear
giant yellow flag
who's doing the treading
exhausting
a not-so-civil war of neighbors with tall fences
fiercely typing
submit share share share

QUESTIONING

what do you remember about the past
specifically

yeah you're using that word wrong
i said laughing

the past isn't specific
it's abstract
it's complex
it's a million hours
very few the same
so asking for specifics
yeah
it would take another lifetime
just to tell you

QUIET

being the part of the totem pole
rotting in soil
is not me
being the backseat driver
kind of sucks
but
it's best to stay
out of things
scalloped tongue
pushing against grinding teeth
clenching my jaw shut

quiet

RACING

sometimes she feels like a gerbil
running around and around
on its wheel
diesel fueled
waiting for the garage to open
it never does
so she revs and revs
massaging the steering wheel in anticipation
she longs to free herself
from the endless preparation
for a race
that feels like it will never come
she begs
open the door

RADICAL

she decided to try
sleeping more
she knew it seemed
like a radical choice
but what did she have to lose
the voice whispered
a few hours a day
you can put toward other things
she shut the voice up
they say i'll live longer
the voice whispered
but you'll be old then
she shrugged
let's just try it

RESPONSIBLE

how do we
take down the bullies
if they
paused
and
took a breath
if they
listened
and
looked with clear eyes
it wouldn't be our responsibility
until then
vigilance

ROUNDER

she was surprised
by the
woman in the mirror
too many changes
too quickly
she wished for a veil
a black veil
to hide
and
to mourn
the person she was

SCARRED

all the women
linked by a cord
no man could understand
generation after generation
tied by blood
leaving its scar
an introduction
of tears and miracles

SELFISH

you always make everything about
you

as soon
as he uttered the words
she thought of
her childhood
taking care of everything to keep her mom happy
and her dad sane

she thought of all the teachers
she strived to make proud

she thought of all the times
she drove a drunk friend home
when she could have been
anywhere else

she thought of giving up dreams for herself
to take care of other people

she thought of the time
she stepped back
so an ex could
step forward

she thought of the house she lost
because she was already working three jobs
and taking care of a toddler
while a different ex
slept in
still drunk

she thought of toxic business partners
she tried to please
clients who were mad
when she answered the phone
and that guy who always stole her parking space

she thought about how
she wanted her daughter to have
better
better
BETTER

and she realized
the only time she ever
thought truly of herself
was in the moment
when she left people behind

she hoped her daughter would grow up to be
selfish

SHAMED

we have all known shame
felt the heat of the flush to our faces
as we recall again
the event
not the embarrassment of others knowing
no
the heat of our own disgust
and we have all known forgiveness
we've looked on others with understanding and grace
and felt others give us the same as we cry inwardly
wondering when the memory might fade
and when we might shrink
so small
that others might forget

SHARP

sharp static
filled her head
not fuzzy
loud
breathing and counting
just made the static
push
back
so she let it run on
forcing her
awake
though her eyes were heavy

SHINY

false friends who promised to be there
for road trips with loud songs
and for forever
who push you away when you need them the most
are painted rocks
shiny for fools
without the weight of true gold
true friends might not agree
but they hold you regardless
their golden weight
a heavy comfortable blanket
of loyalty and commitment and love
never turning their back
time shows you one from the other
always

SPINNING

the water was rising
lightning
whitened the street

thunder on top of it

we were like towels
in a washing machine
sticking to the sides
as the world spun out of control

STICKY

she crawled
through the wreckage
looking for anything
worth saving
knowing
glue wouldn't be enough
but being grateful for it
anyway

STOIC

what if you
talk
and
say
what you
hope
want
need
and no one cares

you cry
when no one is looking
and you keep showing up

stoic

STRUGGLING

i would never tell you who to love
i said
a lie
because i really wanted to tell you
to love me and mine
but that was long ago and
now it seems like i made the moment up
or maybe i shrugged it off
like a snow covered coat
that never fit well
but was already hanging in the closet
left by some previous owner
who laughed at the idea of me
struggling with her
cast off

SWEEPING

the mess of unnecessary bits
frustrated her
and
as her anger grew
she mentally liquidated
until all of it was
clean
simple
pure

she found herself
with a vision
a goal
a purpose

THIN

she wished
for thicker skin
it would be nice
to have things
affect her less

teleporting would be nice too

TWO

she pulled into the gas station
grateful it was there in the middle of nowhere
it was old school no debit card slot
so she wandered into the store

can i help you

an old man
with deep set laugh lines asked
a hint of a rattle in his voice
as if he'd smoked for decades

thirty in the car and a bottle of water
please

he nodded and handed her change
and the water from a clear case next to him

you two traveling far

she smiled
heading to oregon to visit family

always meant to make it that way
i hear the coast is pretty

it is
thanks

as she filled up the tank she realized he'd said

you two

she was traveling
alone

UNAVOIDABLE

time passed
   quicker than i'd wanted
   the days not
   as slow as i'd hoped
   i blinked
   and kids grew
   and so did i
   changing in ways
   unavoidable
   there were mistakes
   but there was
   is
   also a lot of love
   and more to come
   with time

UNBALANCED

clutching a ripped safety net
she touched ground
briefly
long enough to remember
how she felt when she believed
the net was whole
and then she was flung back
back to the frayed tightrope of her life
to balance
knowing there is nothing
truly nothing
to catch her when she inevitably
falls again

UNCOMFORTABLE

she was not at ease with him
her hands shook
she worried
that her hair was a mess
her eyebrows unshaped
her breath too quick
worried that she was too dull
after all who was she
a person with too many worries
and no time
her life not dictated by her own pen
and yet she longed to know him

and she liked her unease

VISIBLE

whenever
she felt invisible
she would
open her front door
and exist again
at home

WASTEFUL

it would have been worth the bad times
if he'd turned out a better man she thought
instead all the time and effort was wasted
she felt sorry for the woman who was trying now
well almost sorry

never waste too much time on a man
she told her daughter
you can only give so much before you start to kick yourself

okay mama the six-year-old agreed
whipped cream from her hot cocoa dusting her nose making
her glow

she wasn't going to let that time be a complete waste

WATCHFUL

she watched
the elderly man
feed the squirrel from his bench
the animal
would run up
and grab the food
stuff it
into his cheek
and run back to eat
keeping his eye on the man

she admired them both
one for his generosity
and the other for its caution

WET

she jumped
into the museum
because of the rain
she was happy to see
that someone was hosting
free wine
(with a donation)
(she put in a dollar)
she took the artist's card
nodding
like she knew what she was
looking at

WINTERING

ridiculous retellings
of the same old story
until nothing sounds new
and the scratching sounds of an old record player
seem to accompany the words

stories wilt
like flowers in the july sun
first they lose luster
then they brown
until pulled or blown away
leaving the seed of
a new story to be planted
fresh dirt in some other yard awaits

WISTFUL

searching
the thrift store racks
she discovered
a skirt she once wore
silky
short
full of colors she no longer wore
she remembered the way
she held herself
graceful
playful
flirty
she touched the light fabric
wistful

Acknowledgments

First, I have to thank my daughter, Rhiannon. Being your mom makes me braver. Your fearless creativity and willingness to fix as you go spilled into me. I might overthink it, but I still follow through because of you.

Tony, your love and encouragement give me the space to create. I'm grateful every day.

Devanie Angel and Angela Taylor, thank you both for all the coaching, proofreading, encouragement, late night messages, and anything else I'm forgetting. Most of all, thanks for going first. I owe you both caffeine.

To my other family and friends, thank you for always showing up for me. The pandemic proved to me I am loved. You bought my art and pushed me forward when you could have shut me out. You'll never know the full extent of my gratitude.